This Book
Belongs to:

. . . .

. . . .

First Edition published in December 2010 by WonderBook Press LLC.
P.O. Box 802184, Santa Clarita, CA 91380-2184

The text in this book is set in Centaur
The illustrations in this book were created using graphite pencil , adobe photoshop and photo collage.

ISBN 978-0-692-00864-5

Library of Congress Control Number: 2010926074

Printed by R.R.Donnelley Dongguan

To find out more about Libby boom, visit www.wonderbookpress.com

by Catherine Rae Purves
illustrations by Tuesday Mourning

wonderbookpress.com

As I fluffed up my pillow
and climbed into bed, a thought
kept on twirling around in my head.

It started right after I finished my prayer.
I wondered if God really knew I was there.
How can He know every person on earth?
How can He track all the billions of births?

I'm going to be baptized tomorrow
at three. And, I'm not so sure He'll
remember me.

I knelt on my bed and looked out at the moon, then whispered to God, “It’s me Libby Boom...

...do you hear me down here on this warm summer night? I’m the girl with big ears and an overbite.”

Not a word from above, not so much as a peep. Then time slowly passed and I dozed off to sleep.

The next thing I knew, I was floating up high. My spirit was free and I wanted to fly. Past my pink curtains and into the night, the city below twinkled sparkly and bright.

It felt like my Dad was holding me close, while lifting me up through a giant cosmos.

I zoomed between planets as stars danced around,
then out of nowhere came a beautiful sound.

Light filled the sky; I felt so much love.
It must be my Father in heaven above.

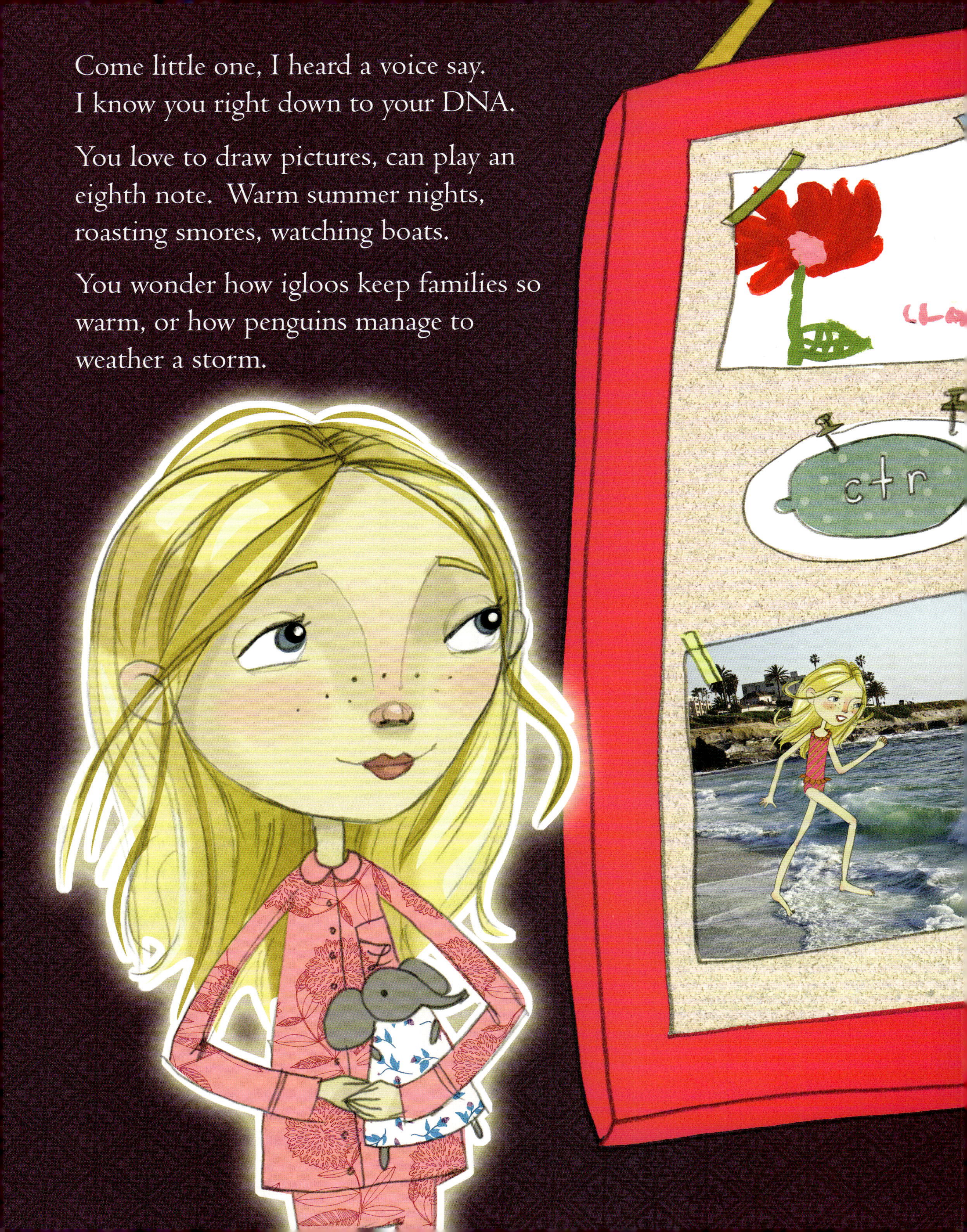

Come little one, I heard a voice say.
I know you right down to your DNA.

You love to draw pictures, can play an eighth note. Warm summer nights, roasting smores, watching boats.

You wonder how igloos keep families so warm, or how penguins manage to weather a storm.

You like to jump waves as they crash on the beach.
You love the first bite of a sweet juicy peach.

You love to take walks on the beach with your mum. And give her a hug when you've done something dumb.

You like to spend time with your Dad at the park. And love when he hums you to sleep in the dark.

You like to dress up like a tree frog and dance. Or wear a beret and pretend you're in France.

I hear every single one of your prayers. I know when you're sad and full of despair.

I know who you are, my sweet little girl. You shine in the dark like a beautiful pearl.

The next thing I knew, I was in His embrace. Gently He brushed all the tears from my face.

"Oh, Heavenly Father," I heard myself say. "I want this forever, oh please let me stay."

Come little one, He whispered so sweet.
There's someone in Ghana I want you meet.

africa
Ghana
Kenya
congo
atlantic ocean
south africa
indian ocean

Kofi is gentle and gives
with his heart.
He's happy and friendly,
helpful and smart.

He likes to play football, the color of blue. His loves chicken stew with a paste called fufu.

His parents would love to send Kofi to school. They know it would give him the right kind of tools.

But most of the time, they must work just to eat. And day in and out, he works hard in the heat.

He prays all the time, he gives thanks for his life. He isn't kept down by his pain or his strife.

Kofi is going to be baptized this year. He dreams of this day and his prayers are sincere.

I know who he is, my sweet little boy, he shines like the sun and exemplifies joy.

Come little one, He whispered so sweet.
There's someone in Hong Kong I want you to meet.

Little Mai Li is funny and sweet, she loves turnip cakes made of sausage and meat.

She has a sweet sister; they've always been close. She has other friends but loves Chun Li the most.

They live on a beautiful street in Hong Kong;
it's crowded and busy (and looks very long).

They love Chinese New Year, the color of red.
Victoria Harbor, the birds overhead.

Mai Li was baptized the seventh of May. I stood there beside her and smiled as they prayed.

I know who she is, my Mai Li so sweet, Her love for the Savior is pure and complete.

Come little one, he whispered so sweet.
There's someone in Tahiti I want you to meet.

Rahi is quiet, thoughtful and strong. He's part of this island -- it's where he belongs.

He loves to watch whales as they come up for air. The blow hole, the jumps - and all the fanfare.

The smell of hibiscus, a shiny black pearl, tropical rain storms, the waves as they curl.

Family home evening and coconut toast --
these are the things Rahi
values the most.

At night as he lays on
the white sugar sand, he
measures the distance
of stars with his hands.

Rahi is going to be baptized today. He's chosen the spot – right here in the bay.

I know who he is -- my little Rahi. The love in his heart is as big as the sea.

Come little one, He said quietly.
I reached for His hand as
He smiled at me.

The things that you've shown me,
I'll never forget. You love every person,
from here to Tibet.

You know all our feelings, our struggles,
our thoughts. You know every detail
(and things we've forgot).

There's no one on earth that you've ever left out. I'm sorry I ever had one little doubt.

I love you completely, He whispered to me.
There's no other person, I'd rather you be.

All that I ask is that you obey.
So, you can be with me in heaven someday.

"That's what a promise is all about. Oh, I want to be baptized,"
I heard myself shout!

The Savior was baptized to show me the way. I'll pray for His guidance and strength everyday.

Life can be tough, and full of heartache, and sometimes I'll struggle and make some mistakes.

You'll give me a gift on my baptism day, a friend who will never lead me astray.

This gift is receiving the Holy Ghost. A sweet gentle voice that I'll treasure the most.

Later that night as I thought of my dream,
I knew in my heart that He'd spoken to me.

You'll never forget me. I know this for sure.
Your love is forever. It's perfectly pure.

I turned on my side and looked out at the moon.
Good night Heavenly Father --

Love Libby Boom.

my baptism date
location
who came